Pansy
Pig

Chris
Rabbit

Henry's
Cat

Sammy
Snail

Denise
Duck

Phillipe
Frog

Ted
Tortoise

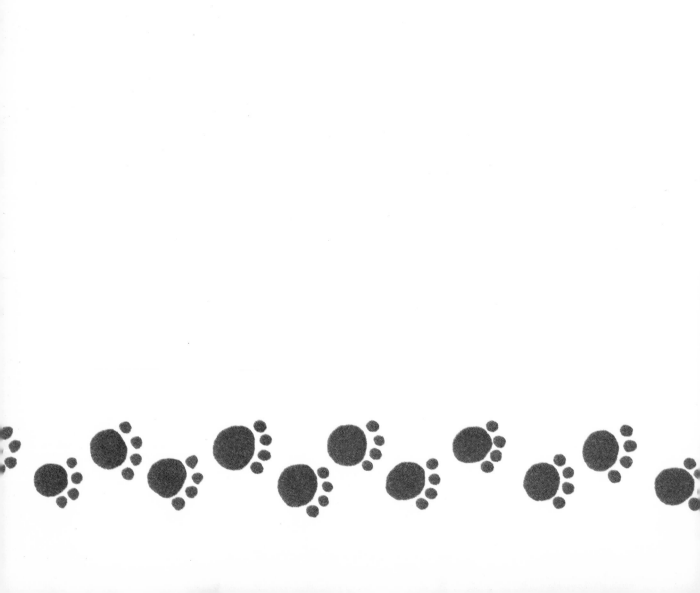

Henry's Cat ©

The Storybook

LITTLE SIMON
Published by Simon & Schuster, Inc., New York

1 2 3 4 5 6 7 8 9 10   ISBN: 0-671-63561-1

CONTENTS

PAGE

The Big Fight

Henry's Cat switched on the TV. He found himself looking at a boxing match with the World Champion. After the fight, the champion said that he earned over a million dollars a year, and that didn't even include lunch money. It seemed like a lot of money, but the interesting thing was that his manager got half of that, and *he* didn't have to fight.

Henry's Cat tried to work out how many doughnuts you could buy for half a million dollars. It was a lot, even if you bought the most expensive kind with three kinds of jelly in them. A boxing manager's job was the sort of job he felt he might be good at. He only needed to persuade someone to go and fight someone else, then collect the money from everyone watching.

Henry's Cat had an idea. He gathered all his friends together and said, "I have a very important announcement to make. Hands up all those who would like to have half a million dollars to spend." Well, of course, they all put their hands up—with the exception of Sammy Snail, who just waggled his tail.

"All you have to do is close your eyes and pick one of these pieces of colored paper out of this hat." Each one took out a bit. They found that there were four colors—two pieces of paper in each color.

Henry's Cat then said, "You have all been fairly matched I see, and now for the next step. Those with the same color will fight a boxing match to decide the winner."

They all felt cheated. Pansy Pig said, "That's not fair. I thought you were going to give us a half a million dollars."

Henry's Cat looked apologetic. "Oh, I'm sorry. I forgot to mention it. First, you have to win the Boxing World Championship, but that will be easy because I'm going to be your manager."

Ted Tortoise said, "It's ten minutes to hibernation time, so that counts me out," and just went back into his shell.

Philippe Frog said French boxing rules required permission from his great-grandfather.

In fact everyone had an excuse, except Chris Rabbit, who actually liked the idea of being the Boxing World Champion.

It was decided that Chris Rabbit would represent them all, and they would cheer him on. He went into training right away. Henry's Cat helped him lose some weight immediately by eating Chris's share of the pudding they were having for dinner.

It was very rigorous training, and included weightlifting, jumping, swimming, shadowboxing, and carrying groceries back to Henry's Cat's house. Chris ran ten miles every morning and knocked on Henry's Cat's door as he passed to report progress.

The local newspaper was very impressed by Chris's successes and printed his photo with a caption saying: "Mystery boxer challenges the world." It also ran a story that Henry's Cat had made up to make it sound a bit more interesting, telling how Chris Rabbit had practiced all winter by shadowboxing with snowmen, and had beaten every one in less than ten rounds, and how he was an expert at karate and could break wood with his bare hands and sharpen pencils with his fingers. And that he would have been chosen for the Olympics, but he was on vacation that day.

After that, Chris Rabbit only had to walk along the road, and everyone recognized him and asked him when he would be fighting for the World Championship. And he would say, "Ask my manager, ask my manager," and point to Henry's Cat. But Henry's Cat said it was a secret in case the opponent found out, but he would sell them a ticket for the big fight, and let them know by Thursday. In this way he sold lots and lots of tickets.

Henry's Cat was now quite confident about winning. When he saw the Boxing World Champion on TV, he wrote a postcard saying, "Dear Boxing World Champion, We are ready when you are. Please meet us behind the bicycle shed after lunch next Thursday. P.S. Please bring a million dollars and a spare set of gloves that we can borrow. Yours sincerely, Henry's Cat."

Henry's Cat put up posters all around the village announcing the big fight. Everyone was very excited about it, and Henry's Cat was sitting in his rocking chair daydreaming of how he would spend the money. His daydreams were rudely shattered by a knock at the door. Officer Bulldog was there with a poster in his hand, which he held up. "And what is this here here here?" he asked.

"It's the big fight we're going to have. Do you want to buy a ticket?" said Henry's Cat. Officer Bulldog looked very serious and tapped his foot.

"No, I do not want a ticket. Don't you know it is against the law to hold parades, carnivals, meetings, and exhibitions in public places without permission from the authorities?" Henry's Cat didn't know. It was all too much for a small cat, especially when he had a Boxing World Championship to organize as well.

"Oh, I'm sorry, Officer Bulldog, can you let me have permission? You can write it on the back of this old laundry list, and that will settle it, won't it?"

It didn't settle it. Officer Bulldog ordered Henry's Cat to take down all the posters and cancel the boxing match. Henry's Cat hurriedly dropped a note to the Boxing World Champion that the fight was off for the time being and not to lose his title to anyone else for the moment. Then Henry's Cat went around and pinned up notices saying that the World Championship fight with Chris Rabbit had been put off due to good weather, and a picnic was replacing it.

Luckily everyone was happy with that, especially when Chris Rabbit gave an exhibition of blindfold boxing and accidentally knocked himself out. Henry's Cat philosophically said, "Well, I didn't get ten rounds of boxing, but I can get ten rounds of drink," and lined himself up ten glasses of lemonade with a piece of cake for each. Everyone thought the picnic was a knockout.

The Invasion

Henry's Cat had just seen a war movie on TV. He wasn't quite sure which war it was, but one of the heroes had trained everyone to be ready in case *they*—the enemy—started something naughty, which *they* did, and which *we* were ready for, all because of the hero.

It seemed a good way to become a hero, and Henry's Cat decided this was as good a way as any. The first thing to do was to convince a few of his friends that *they*—the enemy—might do something at any time and *we* had to be prepared.

First of all, he went up to his grandfather's chest and looked for something suitable for a hero to wear. He found a tin hat, an old gas mask, a book on first aid, two Boy Scout badges for cooking and gardening, a whoopee whistle, a bicycle light, and a book about Morse code. It seemed like enough to cover any emergency. Obviously his grandfather had known that Henry's Cat would be a hero.

The next day, he invited all his friends to the garden. Then, standing up in the wheelbarrow wearing his tin hat, gas mask and Boy Scout badges, he read out of the Morse code book: "Dot, dot, dot. Dash, dash, dash. Dot, dot, dot."

Henry's Cat took off his mask and said, "That is how you say SOS in Morse code, which means 'Send Out Someone' when there is trouble."

"What sort of trouble?" asked Pansy Pig.

"It's in case of war, if *they* invade us. We have to be prepared, and *I* am going to train you all to be heroes when it happens."

"Who are *they*, what do *they* look like, and when are *they* coming, because I'm going away this weekend," said Douglas Dog.

"I can't tell you who *they* are, because it's a military secret, and we don't want the enemy to know that *we* know who *they* are. But I have all their names and addresses here in this envelope, which I will

open as soon as I get word from my superiors." He waved an envelope that was really his gas bill, as he knew he had to keep up the morale of his troops.

"As to what *they* look like, they will of course be disguised—cunning fiends that they are—so if you see anyone looking like someone else, that will be them. In regard to when they will come, you will hear the alarm bell ringing, and you will immediately take action stations and drop everything, apart from eating and sleeping."

Henry's Cat then explained that the key positions of the village were the bakery and the ice cream parlor, as the enemy must be deprived of food supplies at all costs. He said, "We will fight them in the fields and on the beaches..."

"And by the duck pond!" added Denise Duck, showing true patriotism.

"And two doors down from the burger restaurant!" said Mosey Mouse, getting into the spirit of the thing.

"Yes. We will start training tomorrow. I personally promise you that for every two medals you win you will get one free, or ten percent off your next purchase. I can't be fairer than that, can I?" said Henry's Cat. They all went home to get whatever weapons they could find, to be fully prepared for when *they* came. Henry's Cat put on his gas mask again and whistled the national anthem as he saluted, then went inside and had an extra-large helping of victory pie, which he had baked for the occasion.

The next day they all assembled in front of Henry's Cat's house. Henry's Cat blew his whoopee whistle to get their attention and explained that they would now be learning marching, signaling, assault tactics, camouflage, and making sandbags. As a special hardship test, no one would have anything to eat until lunchtime, and even then, only three extra helpings of apple pie would be allowed.

It was a hard course; but with determination and encouragement all of them, with the exception of Sammy Snail, passed the test. Sammy Snail was put on civilian duty as lookout, while the rest lined up for inspection. Henry's Cat marched past them slowly and inspected them in detail. He was proud of his gallant team, ready, willing and able to take on the defense of their neighborhood, without thought of personal safety or reward.

Henry's Cat then said, "To stop spies from sneaking in, we will have a secret password, which is 'carrots.' Anyone who doesn't answer to this must be considered an enemy until further notice."

Nothing happened for over a week. Henry's Cat wondered if his work had been in vain—and with it his hopes of being a hero. But one night Sammy Snail, always on the alert, rushed as fast as his foot would take him and shouted, "The alarm bell is ringing, the alarm bell is ringing."

Henry's cat jumped out of bed, only stopping for a bowl of cornflakes and two apple pancakes with hamburger sauce. They all assembled outside Henry's Cat's house under the midnight sky. Following Sammy Snail as slowly as they could, they reached the woods and could hear the bell ringing. In the dark shadows it was difficult to tell friend from foe, so they kept saying "carrots" to each other, just to be on the safe side. But then they saw a dark and suspicious figure creeping through the woods stealthily, carrying a rope. Without a doubt, the invasion had started.

With the shout of "Geronimo" they pulled the figure to the ground. Then, taking the rope from the enemy's hand, they quickly bound him up into a bundle.

Henry's Cat felt *very* pleased indeed. On his very first encounter with the enemy he had single-handedly—with the help of his team— stopped the invasion and saved the country from perils unknown. Leaving Sammy Snail to stand guard, the rest marched back to the police station, where Officer Bulldog was on night duty and just having his midnight cocoa.

"Officer Bulldog, we have to report that the enemy has attacked but has been defeated by my team of gallant friends. He is awaiting your disposal at your earliest convenience, sir," said Henry's Cat, saluting.

Officer Bulldog was a bit taken by surprise and knocked over his cocoa while getting out his notebook. They all turned and marched out, with him following and making notes on the way. They soon arrived back and, having said "carrots" to Sammy Snail, they proceeded with the interrogation.

Officer Bulldog looked at the tied-up bundle and said, "I am given to understand that you, an enemy of unknown identity, have, with intent and aforethought, caused a disturbance by invading our area without due permission.

Henry's Cat folded his arms and looked at the bundle. This would teach *them* a lesson they wouldn't forget.

But the bundle answered in a very angry voice, "Grrrrr, get me out of here. I'm Farmer Giles. Someone will pay for this, without a doubt."

Well, it seemed that the alarm bell was the one around Daisy the Cow's neck, and Farmer Giles had got a rope to bring her in after she had wandered off. Officer Bulldog understood the mistake and said it was all in hand. He untied Farmer Giles and sent him home, then took the rather sorry-looking heroes back to the police station.

He said that he appreciated the initiative, courage, and decisive action Henry's Cat and his team had taken. But in such matters the President should have the first crack at catching the enemy. Otherwise there wasn't much point in being President, was there? He took their names and addresses should they ever be needed.

Officer Bulldog then gave them all a cup of cocoa and some jelly doughnuts to cheer them up.

Chris Rabbit said, "Never mind, never mind; people are always losing wars. Perhaps we can find one of them."

Henry's Cat thought about it and said, "If I find a war, I'll bring it to the police station and claim the reward." And with that, he helped himself to another large jelly doughnut.

The Magician

Henry's Cat was watching a very interesting program on television. Lots of magicians came on and did all sorts of tricks, like taking flowers out of hats, making golf balls disappear into their ears, and even tearing up money and making it whole again. It was very clever, but there was one trick that was better than all of these. Sawing a lady in half.

The lady got into a long box. Then the magician rolled up his sleeves to show there was nothing up them—except his arms, of course—and then he started to saw the box in half. Henry's Cat held his breath. It just wasn't possible. But the magician pulled both parts of the box apart, then put them back together, and the lady got out and blew kisses to everyone, and they all clapped very loudly.

Several days later Henry's Cat was walking past a bookstore and saw in the window a book by the very same magician. The title was *How to Be a Magician in Six Easy Lessons.* Well, it was too good an opportunity to miss. He bought the book, then hurried home as fast as he could.

He read, "The first thing to learn is how to say the magic words. 'Abracadabra sim sala bim.' These words must be practiced one hundred times a day, and you must remember them even with your eyes closed and your hands behind your back."

"Mmmm," said Henry's Cat, "I can see this is not going to be easy, but practice makes perfect." He walked around the house saying, "Abracadabra sim sala bim," and expecting something to disappear. But nothing did.

The second chapter said, "Be relaxed at all times." Ah, that's it, thought Henry's Cat. So he went for a little walk to relax, practicing his magic words with his eyes shut and his hands behind his back.

Of course, it was not long before he bumped into someone. He opened his eyes and found it was Chris Rabbit. "Hello," said Chris.

"Abracadabra sim sala bim," said Henry's Cat.

"What's that?" said Chris.

"It's magic. I'm practicing magic words so that I can saw people in half, like they do on television," said Henry's Cat.

"Oh," said Chris, "yes, that's very useful."

It struck Henry's Cat that if he actually did become a magician, he would need an assistant. These tended to be ladies who were suitable for sawing in half, but it might be far more interesting to see a rabbit sawed in half.

"I've got an idea, Chris. Why don't you and I practice together? You can be my assistant, since I'm the one who has the book."

Chris thought about it and then said, "All right, but no putting rabbits in hats."

They went back to Henry's Cat's house and started to practice magic
words. After a while, Chris became a bit bored and drifted off to sleep.
When Henry's Cat noticed this, an idea occurred to him. While Chris
was asleep, he would practice cutting a rabbit in half. If he did it
quickly and put him back again, Chris would never know.

Henry's Cat hurried off to get a saw and a long box. He brought
these back, and then put Chris in the box by carefully lifting up his legs
and slipping them in one end. Then, getting his magic book, he looked
up the chapter on sawing ladies in half. It said, "Place lady in suitable
box and close lid. Proceed to saw box in half while saying magic
words." It all seemed quite easy. He proceeded to saw the box in half,

but very quietly, because it can be very upsetting to wake up and find yourself being sawed in half, even by a friend.

It was not long before the box was sawed right through, and Chris was still sleeping soundly. Now to put him back again, thought Henry's Cat. He looked in the magic book again and saw for the first time a note in small letters. "Do not attempt this trick until you have mastered Chapter Five." He flipped back to Chapter Five, but that said, "Do not attempt this trick until you have mastered Chapter Four." He had to go right back to the beginning to work out how to put Chris back together again. "Oh, dear," sighed Henry's Cat. "I'd better make a cup of tea and just read through it," which he did.

But, unknown to Henry's Cat, Chris was having a funny dream. He started to twitch a little and then began to sleepwalk. Well, can you imagine what it's like trying to walk when you have been sawed in half? His legs got out of the box and started to walk around. At first they bumped into things, but after a while they found their way out of the door and into the street.

Having walked a little way, Chris's legs stood for a while, leaning against a post. It happened to be a bus stop, and a nice old lady who was standing there helped the legs onto the bus and even paid the fare, which was only half fare for half a rabbit.

After a few stops, the legs got off and walked along and into a field. Well, it's difficult to say whether a pair of legs can get lost. These legs thought they were going to a dance, because that was what Chris was dreaming about. Then as they started dancing around, there was a

loud shout. It was Farmer Giles. The legs were dancing on his cabbages and flattening them. He was very angry and grabbed hold of the tail and hauled the legs back to the road. Just at that moment he saw Officer Bulldog coming along on his rounds. "Aaaaargh! It's lucky I've seen you, Officer. This here pair of legs has been dancing on my cabbages and flattening them."

Well, Officer Bulldog was a bit surprised, but he acted in a very policemanlike way and said, "Leave it to me, Farmer Giles. I'll take them back for questioning," and he took the legs firmly by the tail and marched them off to the police station.

In the meantime, Henry's Cat had read some more of the book, and he went back into the room to put Chris together again. But as he did, Chris started to wake up. "I've had such a funny dream about dancing. I thought I was dancing on cabbages and..."What's this box doing?" he asked.

"Oh, er...the box. Yes, well, it's just a little trick I was trying... actually sawing a lady in half..."

"You...are about to saw me in half?" asked Chris, very surprised.

"Oh, no. I'm not about to saw you in half," said Henry's Cat. "I already have."

Then Chris looked inside the box. He became very confused when he saw what he saw, or didn't see—his legs. "And *where* are my legs, which you have sawed off?"

Henry's Cat stood still for a moment, not daring to look. Then, he started to look under the table, chairs, everywhere. "Well, they were there a little while ago. Perhaps if you whistle for them, they'll come back."

"Don't be silly," said Chris. "They don't have any ears."

"I'll go out and see if I can find them. Don't go away."

Luckily, Officer Bulldog was coming back with Chris's legs held firmly by the tail. Henry's Cat said, "Excuse me, Officer Bulldog, you don't happen to have seen a pair of legs walking around by themselves, do you...like the ones you have there?"

"As a matter of fact I have, and a very naughty pair of legs they are. Been dancing on Farmer Giles's cabbage patch, they have. If you know anything about them, you'd better come back to the police station as a witness."

When they got there, Officer Bulldog got out a pen and a big book.

"Now, when did you lose this pair of legs you are looking for?"

"About an hour ago, when I was sawing Chris Rabbit in half, as a magic trick."

"Sawing Chris Rabbit in half," as he wrote in the book. "Are they your legs?" said Officer Bulldog.

"They belong to Chris Rabbit. I've got to take them back to him."

"I can't let them leave until I have proof of who they belong to."

Henry's Cat ran out of the station and was soon back with Chris in a wheelbarrow. "There you are," said Henry's Cat. "You can see they belong to him now, can't you?"

"Seeing is not always believing, as people who get up to magic tricks should know," said Officer Bulldog. "Do you have a certificate stating these legs belong to you and that they have been acquired legally?"

Well, it was a problem. Then Henry's Cat had a brilliant idea. Officer Bulldog nodded very seriously, then led the legs into another room, with Henry's Cat, and stood in the doorway so that Chris could not see what was going on. Officer Bulldog then raised his hand and said to Henry's Cat, "One, two, three, go," and almost immediately Chris Rabbit started giggling and saying, "Stop, stop, stop."

34

"All right, that's enough," said Officer Bulldog. "If you'll just sign here, you can take the legs away with you, but don't let me catch them dancing on the cabbages again."

On the way home Henry's Cat said, "That was a good idea of mine to tickle your feet as proof that these are your legs, wasn't it?" Chris agreed, but was worried about Henry's Cat putting him together again. When they got home, Chris got back into the box with his legs, while Henry's Cat said in a very loud voice, "Abracadabra, hocum pocum, sin sala bim," and showed Chris that there was nothing up his sleeves.

It worked very well. Chris got out of the box with his legs on properly. He felt so relieved that he forgave Henry's Cat. They had dinner together and decided that magic was better left to magicians, though Chris said, "Just one more disappearing trick. Close your eyes," and as Henry's Cat did so, Chris ate all the ice cream.

The Television Commercial

It was such a beautiful day that Henry's Cat felt it must be someone's birthday—a good reason to celebrate. He couldn't think whose birthday it could be, but he decided that perhaps it would come to him later, and he should just get on with celebrating it.

He wondered what was the right way to celebrate the birthday of someone you haven't thought of yet. It couldn't be a "for-he's-a-jolly-good-fellow" sort of birthday or anything like that. It would have to be a sneaking-up-on-it sort of birthday that you celebrate rather quietly by yourself without telling anyone. It needed that sort of food as well—and he had just the thing.

He went to his cupboard and took out a large carton, inside which was a brown cardboard box, inside which was a plastic bag, inside which was a paper package, inside which was a glass jar, inside which was his greatest delight—a can of Snoggles Special Cat Food!

He held the can out at arm's length and admired it. This treat was so special that Henry's Cat could not afford it. It had been a Christmas gift that he had saved for just such an occasion.

He put it back in the plastic bag and got ready to go to the park and eat it very slowly with a small spoon and then just lie in the sun with his eyes closed, and say "Happy birthday" to whoever it was. He would have remembered by that time.

Henry's Cat walked around the park looking for just the right bench under a shady tree and with a nice view. He soon found one. He carefully put his bag down and made himself comfortable, then slowly took out his can of Snoggles Special Cat Food and put it on the seat.

He looked at it and licked his lips, then opened it and took his first spoonful...mmmmmmmmm, it was so delicious. It was a bit like hot chocolate and cinnamon toast when you've just come in from the cold. On the other hand, it was also a bit like hot dogs and baked beans when you've been working hard and missed lunch.

The more Henry's Cat thought about it the more it seemed similar to all the things he liked, and it was like eating them all at once. A beautiful smile spread across his face as he lay back with his eyes closed in the warm sun and said "Happy birthday" to himself.

His blissful state didn't last very long. Someone poked him in the ribs rather hard. Panic swept over Henry's Cat. Was he being robbed?

But the man, who was wearing dark glasses and smoking a big cigar, smiled, and held his hand out to shake Henry's Cat's paw. With mixed feelings, Henry's Cat held one paw out to be shaken while using the other to hide his cat food behind his back.

"I notice you were eating Snoggles Special Cat Food," said the man, flicking his cigar ash all over Henry's Cat in a nonchalant way. "And you looked so satisfied, I just had to meet you. My name is Bertram B. Sneep, and I advertise Snoggles Special Cat Food on television. I would like you to be in our commercial. How would you like that, eh?"

"Oh," said Henry's Cat, not knowing quite what to say to such a thing. "And we'll give you a year's supply of Snoggles Special Cat Food."

A year's supply would last Henry's Cat at least two months if he ate with a small spoon, and only on somebody's birthday. It seemed too good an opportunity to miss.

"Here's my card. Come and see me tomorrow." With that the man shook his cigar ash over Henry's Cat once more and then walked off.

Henry's Cat looked at the card. It said: "Bertram B. Sneep, Chief Advertiser of Snoggles Special Cat Food." There was no doubt about it; it had not been a dream. He quickly ate up the rest of the food in the can. He had to get into practice.

The next day, Henry's Cat put on his very best running shoes and ran all the way to Mr. Sneep's advertising agency.

"You're late," said Mr. Sneep. "We'd better get started," and with that he took Henry's Cat into a big studio where lots of cans of Snoggles Special Cat Food were piled up everywhere.

Mr. Sneep gave Henry's Cat a script, which said, "Snoggles Special Cat Food is very good. I always eat it, even when I'm not hungry. It contains vitamin T and vitamin W for healthy tails and whiskers. Get some today!"

"When you've read it, eat some cat food, and then sit back and smile like you did in the park," explained Mr. Sneep.

Henry's Cat nodded. It sounded very easy. He stood behind a table and started eating the cat food. He was just about halfway through and feeling blissful when Mr. Sneep said, "Okay, take one," and someone clapped two boards together, and the cameras started whirring.

When he had finished doing the commercial, Henry's Cat sat back and lazily ate the rest of the can of food, but Mr. Sneep said, "That took too long. Make it a bit faster. Okay, take two," and they did it again.

This time Mr. Sneep said, "You left out 'vitamin T and vitamin W for healthy tails.' Okay, take three."

Well, eating Snoggles Special Cat Food was blissful until the fifteenth try, by which time Henry's Cat was on his tenth can. After that, it was not quite so blissful. Mr. Sneep complained that Henry's Cat did not have quite the same smile as he'd had in the park.

"You'll have to give me a few minutes to work up an appetite again," said Henry's Cat. He was spurred on by the thought of all the cat food he could have, but he had run out of tummy space.

The next take was just too much. Henry's Cat collapsed in a heap looking rather cross-eyed and holding his tummy. He looked quite ill, and felt even worse. He could just about hear Mr. Sneep speaking very angrily, then suddenly being very happy and saying, "That's it, that's it! Okay, go home."

Henry's Cat didn't remember much more, but he woke up the next day in the hospital, where he had been all night just for a checkup. He was fine now and was allowed to go home, but the doctors advised him not to eat too much.

When he arrived home he found a case of Snoggles Special Cat Food waiting outside his door. He couldn't face it, so he hurried inside and switched on the TV, hoping to forget all about yesterday. He had hardly turned it on when the commercials started. Of all things, it had to be an ad for Snoggles Special Cat Food! Mr. Sneep came on and said, "Why look like this?" He pointed to a very sick-looking Henry's Cat lying on the floor. "When you can be a healthy, fit cat by eating Snoggles Special Cat Food," and he held up a can with a picture of a smiling cat on it.

Just the sight of more Snoggles Special Cat Food made Henry's Cat feel very ill indeed. He clutched his tummy and said, "Uurrgghhhh uk!" and closed his eyes.

It was then he remembered whose birthday he had been celebrating. It was Napoleon's, and he also remembered what Napoleon had said: "An army marches on its stomach." Very apt, thought Henry's Cat, as he lay on his stomach and slowly crawled to bed where he stayed...for the rest of the day, hoping that he wouldn't dream about Snoggles Special Cat Food.